ATHENEUM BOOKS FOR YOUNG READERS ✠ An imprint of Simon & Schuster Children's Publishing Division✠ 1230 Avenue of the Americas ✠ New York, New York 10020 ✠ Copyright © 2012 by Calef Brown ✠ All rights reserved, including the right of reproduction in whole or in part in any form ✠ ATHENEUM BOOKS FOR YOUNG READERS is a registered trademark of Simon & Schuster, Inc. ✠ For more information about special discounts for bulk purchases, please contact Simon & Schuster Special Sales at 1-866-506-1949 or business@simonandschuster.com. ✠ The Simon & Schuster Speakers Bureau can bring authors to your live event. For more information or to book an event, contact the Simon & Schuster Speakers Bureau at 1-866-248-3049 or visit our website at www.simonspeakers.com. ✠ Book design by Debra Sfetsios-Conover ✠ The text of this book is set in Caslon Antique. ✠ The illustrations for this book are rendered in Acrylic. ✠ Manufactured in China ✠ 0412 SCP ✠ First Edition ✠ 10 9 8 7 6 5 4 3 2 1 ✠ Library of Congress Cataloging-in-Publication Data ✠ Brown, Calef. ✠ Pirateria : the wonderful plunderful pirate emporium / Calef Brown. — 1st ed. ✠ p. cm. ✠ Summary: Illustrations and rhyming text invite the reader to explore a store that provides everything a privateer, mutineer, or buccaneer might want in the way of high-quality pirate gear, from clothing to classes in smuggling molasses. ✠ ISBN 978-1-4169-7878-7 (hardcover) ✠ ISBN 978-1-4424-3897-2 ✠ [1. Stories in rhyme. 2. Stores, Retail—Fiction. 3. Pirates—Fiction.] I. Title. ✠ PZ8.3.B8135Pir 2012 ✠ [E]—dc23 ✠ 2011034023

To Connor—
Little swashbuckler
of the redwoods
—C. B.

PIRATERIA

THE WONDERFUL ☠ PLUNDERFUL ☠ PIRATE EMPORIUM

Atheneum Books for Young Readers
New York   London   Toronto   Sydney   New Delhi

Written and illustrated by

CALEF BROWN

Are you a privateer?
A mutineer?
Or just a happy-go-lucky
buccaneer?
Do you need top-quality pirate gear?
Well, never fear,
Pirateria is here!

Our glorious pirate emporium
is known the world over,
from the Spanish Main
to the cliffs of Dover.

From the Barbary Coast
to the shores of Oregon,
just ask Bluebeard or Cap'n Morgan—
they know the score.
Pirateria is the number one pirate store!

Are your sea legs limber?
Your timbers shivered?
No lily-livered landlubbers allowed here!
Pirateria caters to barnacle scrapers
and hull scrubbers,
treasure seekers and sea robbers,
from far-off ports of call.

Gnarly pirates, wall to wall!

What, you ask,
do we sell?

Well . . .

We have treasure chests—the very best.
Head rags, vests, and black pantaloons;
satchels and pouches
for gems and doubloons.
Spinnakers, jibs, and rope in hanks;
solid maple walking planks.
At the end of aisle nine
there's fresh lime quinine
to ward off the scurvy
while toiling at sea.

Buy one galleon, get one free!

Ahoy there, you salty dogs!
Cast off those grog-stained pirate togs.
Unlike fancy haberdashers,
we sell duds for saber clashers.

So climb that rigging
and dig for ingots
hidden on deserted beaches!
You can't beat our breeches!
They'll last a lifetime,
and the pockets will hold
all the gold you can carry.

(Though it must be told:
Pirates' lifetimes may vary.)

Do you need some strong luggage?
Some good sturdy bags?
Join our very best customers:
seafaring scallywags.

They love our ditty bags, adore our duffels—
perfect for stuffing with big ruffles,
and clothes of all types,
including those stripey shirts pirates like.

Be on the lookout for specials
in our weekly dispatches.
And this just in:
a fresh batch of eye patches!
Two per package
to prevent mismatches.

BRiny deep
GREEN

bilge water
gray

scurvy
scarlet

pillage
orange

cannonball
black

swashbuckled
huckleberry

plunder
plum

moby
white

dreaded
red

Pirates love surprises.
They often need disguises
for ambushes and sneak attacks.
We have stacks and stacks
of fake mustaches and beards
in many eccentric hues—
ruby reds and electric blues,
as well as the classic
Blackbeard black.

Does it look weird?

Take it back!

The Yo Ho Hosiery
and Footwear department
has a huge assortment
of big buckled shoes.
Who can choose?

Buy yourself an extra,
in case you lose one
(or give it to Long John Silver,
he can probably use one).

Most pirates
expect to be shipwrecked,
so protect yourself
and stay connected
with Pirateria brand message bottles.
They come in three models
for every SOS need.

Note: Rescue neither implied nor guaranteed.

Sharp-eyed sea rovers
go overboard
for our sword selection.
Have you seen the new cutlasses?
Great for sticking into atlases
to mark a spot.
What else is hot?
Matching scimitar
and scabbard sets
for swashbucklers
and swashbucklerettes.

Avast, ye fast mast climbers!
These handy brass timers
will help you set a new record,
then best it.
Take one to the top
and test it!

Did you know
that the all-time champ
has a hook for a hand?
He likes to rest
in the crow's nest
and look for land.

Pirateria is not just a store.
Oh no, ho ho,
there's so much more.
We provide night classes
on smuggling molasses
and making your own spyglasses.

Learn the hidden dangers
of shoals and shallows.
Get useful tips
on avoiding the gallows.
Do you know the ins and outs
of charts and compasses?
Or protecting your booty
during wild pirate rumpuses?
Sign up now
at one of our many campuses!

Attention
buckos, oafs, and toughs.
You'll walk the plank
if we spy fisticuffs.
Whenever you spot
your pirate nemesis
on our premises,
be a good sport.
Declare a truce,
then hunt for grub
in the food court.

Any questions?
Our helpful sales staff
may look like riffraff
and need a quick bath,
but despite being gruff
they know their stuff,
and all speak fluent pirate jargon.
At Pirateria
we put the "arg"
in "bargain"!

So remember,
whether you need
a Jolly Roger,
a treasure map,
or just a feather for your cap,
Pirateria is *the* most wonderful,
plunderful pirate supermart!
Look alive and do your part—
visit our newest location
down by the ocean
on the winding path
behind the wisteria.

Set your sails
for
Pirateria!

FIN